Extra! Extra!
Kitty-Cat Mishap!

Mr. Banner added, "If it's okay with all your parents, I could use three eight-year-old extras in *The Aliens Next Door*. What do you say?"

"Yes!" Nancy squealed. "Please, Dad, can we?"

Mr. Drew laughed. "Sounds like fun. George and Bess, I'll give your parents a call and see if it's okay with them."

"Yay!" The three girls cheered.

Mr. Banner opened his mouth to say something. But he was interrupted by a loud, horrible screech.

Nancy spun around. "What was that?" she cried out as something went tearing past them.

It was a cat. Nancy recognized her; it was Fluffington! Except Fluffington wasn't beautiful and fluffy and white, like she was in the Krunchies commercials. She was covered with blue paint!

Join the CLUE CREW
& solve these other cases!

NANCY DREW

AND THE CLUE CREW™

#8

Lights, Camera . . . Cats!

BY CAROLYN KEENE

ILLUSTRATED BY MACKY PAMINTUAN

Aladdin Paperbacks
New York   London   Toronto   Sydney

visit us at www.abdopublishing.com

Reinforced library bound edition published in 2010 by Spotlight, a division of the ABDO Group, 8000 West 78th Street, Edina, Minnesota 55439. Published by agreement with Aladdin Paperbacks, an imprint of Simon & Schuster Children's Publishing Division.

ALADDIN PAPERBACKS
An imprint of Simon & Schuster Children's Publishing Division
1230 Avenue of the Americas, New York, NY 10020
Text copyright © 2007 by Simon & Schuster, Inc.
Illustrations copyright © 2007 by Macky Pamintuan. All rights reserved, including the right of reproduction in whole or in part in any form. ALADDIN PAPERBACKS, NANCY DREW, NANCY DREW AND THE CLUE CREW, and colophon are registered trademarks of Simon & Schuster, Inc. Designed by Lisa Vega

Library of Congress Cataloging-in-Publication Data

This title was previously cataloged with the following information:
Keene, Carolyn.
   Lights, camera...cats! / Carolyn Keene.
    p. cm. -- (Nancy Drew and the Clue Crew ; #8)
   I. Title. II. Series: Nancy Drew and the clue crew ; #8.

[Fic]--dc22   2007921781

ISBN 978-1-59961-645-2 (reinforced library bound edition)

All Spotlight books have reinforced library binding and are manufactured in the United States of America.

CONTENTS

Lights, Camera . . . Cats!

CHAPTER ONE

Hooray for Hollywood

"I can't believe we're in Hollywood!" Nancy Drew said excitedly.

"I can't wait to see all the movie studios," her best friend George Fayne added.

"I can't wait to see all the movie *stars*," said Nancy's other best friend, Bess Marvin. "I packed my autograph book so I can get zillions of autographs!"

The three girls were sitting in the backseat of a shiny silver convertible, heading down West Sunset Boulevard. Nancy's father, Carson Drew, was in the front seat, driving. Next to Mr. Drew was the Drews' housekeeper, Hannah Gruen. "Housekeeper" didn't quite describe

1

Hannah, though. She had been like a mom to Nancy since Nancy's mother died five years ago.

Mr. Drew was in Hollywood on business. He was a lawyer, and one of his clients, Brett Banner, was a movie director. Mr. Drew had decided to combine his work trip with a family vacation and bring Nancy and Hannah along. He had told Nancy that she could invite George and Bess.

The five of them had landed at Los Angeles International Airport less than an hour ago. Now they were cruising through Hollywood in a convertible, with the top down. *What could be more fun?* Nancy thought. She loved the way the wind blew through her long reddish-blond hair. She loved feeling the warm sun on her face.

She also loved the scenery. As they drove, they passed pastel-colored houses with red tile roofs and lush gardens full of tropical flowers.

They saw funky boutiques and outdoor cafés packed with people. They rode by tall palm trees and giant billboards. One of the billboards said: WELCOME TO CALIFORNIA!

"We're almost at our hotel," Mr. Drew called over his shoulder. "It's in a part of Los Angeles called Beverly Hills, which is very close to Hollywood."

3

"Our hotel has five swimming pools," Nancy told George and Bess. "Five!"

"We can each have our own swimming pool," George joked.

"Let's check in, and then we can take a dip," Hannah suggested.

"Later this afternoon, we're invited to visit Thunderchickens Studios," Mr. Drew told everyone. "That's the studio where my client, Mr. Banner, is shooting his latest movie. It's called *The Aliens Next Door*. We'll get a tour and meet the star of the movie."

"Yay!" Nancy exclaimed.

"Awesome," George agreed.

"I'm definitely bringing my autograph book," Bess added.

Mr. Drew chuckled. "You might have a hard time getting an autograph from this particular star, Bess."

"Why, Dad?" Nancy asked, puzzled.

"You'll see," Mr. Drew said mysteriously.

Thunderchickens Studios was a massive complex of buildings on the outskirts of Hollywood. Mr. Drew, Hannah, Nancy, George, and Bess checked in with a security guard at the front gate. The guard gave them all name tags to wear around their necks.

"Mr. Banner is in Soundstage Number Three, to your left," the security guard told them. "They're not in lock up right now, so you can go on in."

"Soundstage? Lock up? What do those words mean?" Nancy asked the guard.

"A soundstage is another name for a building they make movies in," the guard explained. "A lock up is when they're about to shoot a scene, so they have to make sure no one enters the soundstage who isn't supposed to."

Nancy and the others thanked the guard and proceeded to Soundstage #3. As they passed through the heavy metal doors, Nancy felt like jumping up and down. She was about to enter a real-live movie studio.

And what a place it was! The large room—the size of the gym at Nancy's school—was filled with cameras, lights, microphones, cables, and other equipment. In the middle of the room was a fake living room complete with furniture, a TV set, and walls covered with artwork and photographs. A man and a woman were sitting on the couch while another woman with a clipboard stood over them, talking. Other people rushed around, shouting orders and looking very busy.

The woman with the clipboard glanced up when she heard Nancy and her group enter. She was tall and slender, with reddish-brown hair and glasses.

She waved and came over. "Hello, welcome!" she called out. "You must be the Drews. I'm Yasmine, Brett Banner's assistant."

Mr. Drew introduced himself, Nancy, Hannah, George, and Bess. "It's very kind of Brett to let us visit the set," he said.

"Oh, it's no problem," Yasmine said pleasantly. "He's in his office on an overseas call right now. Why don't I give you a quick tour while he wraps it up?"

"Thank you, we would love that," Hannah answered.

"I don't know how much you know about the movie," Yasmine said. "It's called *The Aliens Next Door*. It's a comedy about a family that moves in next door to the Mitchell family, owners of Fluffington. Fluffington is the only one who can tell that the new family, the Graysons, and their dog, Pompom, are actually aliens posing as earthlings."

"Fluffington?" Bess gasped. "As in, Fluffington, the most famous cat in the whole wide world?"

CHAPTER TWO

A Big Blue Mess

"Are you talking about the superfamous Fluffington from the Krunchies cat food commercials?" Nancy asked Yasmine.

Yasmine grinned. "The one and only."

Nancy smiled at her father. No wonder he had said Bess would have a hard time getting an autograph from the star of the movie. The star of the movie was a cat!

"Fluffington is so awesome in the Krunchies commercials," George piped up. "My favorite is the one where her kitty soccer team wins a tournament, and they get a huge trophy full of Krunchies."

"Well, you can all meet Fluffington herself as

soon as she's done with her grooming session," Yasmine said. "One of the groomers is combing and brushing her for her next scene. In the meantime, why don't I introduce you to some of the *humans* on our set."

"Sounds great," Mr. Drew said.

Nancy noticed a big yellow cat dashing behind a potted plant. "That's not Fluffington, is it?" she said, confused. "I thought Fluffington was white."

"That cat is a stray who hangs out here sometimes," Yasmine explained. "We call him Honey Mustard. He's kind of unusual, because he has six toes on each paw."

"That's a lot of toes," Bess said.

Yasmine proceeded to lead them around

the studio. She introduced them to the actors who played Mr. and Mrs. Mitchell, followed by the actors who played the "alien" family, the Graysons. Pompom, a small silver poodle who was the doggie star of the show, was sitting on "Mrs. Grayson's" lap.

Yasmine also introduced them to a young guy with curly black hair who was sitting in front of a fancy-looking computer. "This is Tucker Diaz, our CGI guy," Yasmine said.

"What does CGI stand for?" Bess asked him.

"Computer generated imagery," Tucker replied. "You girls see the movie *Pigs in Space*?"

"That was a totally awesome movie!" George said.

"Well, those pigs weren't really pigs. They were images created by people like me on their computers," Tucker said. "You know how your parents take home movies of you on their video cameras? Imagine if you could create a dinosaur on your computer and add it to one of your parents' movies. It would look like you were hanging out with a dinosaur in your very own backyard, right? Well, that's what I do."

"Cool," Bess said.

"For this movie, I'm creating a whole bunch of computer images of Fluffington and Pom-pom," Tucker went on. "For example, there's a scene where Fluffington goes flying through the air and crashes into a wall. Ouch! I'm creating a computer image of Fluffington flying and crashing so the *real* Fluffington doesn't have to." He added, "When you see the movie, you won't be able to tell the difference between the real Fluffington and the computer generated Fluffington."

"Wow," Nancy said.

Tucker lowered his voice. "I'm trying to convince Mr. Banner to forget about Fluffington and Pompom altogether and use nothing but computer images of them. Animal actors are too unpredictable. Computers are way more reliable." He patted the top of his computer, as though he were petting a cat.

"Tucker," Yasmine said with a frown.

Nancy glanced at Yasmine, then at Tucker. She wondered why Yasmine seemed unhappy about what Tucker had just said.

Yasmine gestured to Mr. Drew and Hannah. "Why don't we move on? Brett should be done with his call by now."

"Terrific," Mr. Drew said.

They all said good-bye to Tucker. Yasmine led them past two actors rehearsing a scene and over to a corner office. The door was closed.

Yasmine knocked. "Brett?" she called out.

The door opened. Brett Banner was tall, tanned, and bald. He was dressed in black jeans and a pink T-shirt with a cartoon picture of a chicken on it. He wore a fancy-looking gold watch on his wrist.

"Yes, yes, I'll have to get back to you on that," Mr. Banner said into a tiny cell phone. Then he snapped it shut and extended his hand to Mr. Drew. "Carson! It's good of you to come all the way out to California. Who are these lovely people you brought along? Introduce me!"

Mr. Drew shook Mr. Banner's hand. He introduced Hannah, Nancy, George, and Bess.

Mr. Banner smiled at the three girls. "How old are you? Twenty? Twenty-five?" he joked.

Nancy giggled. "We're eight."

"We're in third grade," Bess added.

"Third grade. Hmm, well." Mr. Banner looked thoughtful. "It just so happens that we need three third-graders as extras for the movie. Do you know what extras are?"

"Like when my dad gives me extra whipped cream on my ice cream?" George said.

Mr. Banner nodded. "Yes! Extras are like extra actors in the movie, except they don't have to act. Have you ever seen a scene in a movie where there's a big crowd in the background?"

Bess nodded. "In *Pigs in Space*, there was a big crowd in the high school parking lot watching the pig spaceships land."

"Exactly! All those people in that crowd were extras." Mr. Banner added, "If it's okay with all your parents, I could use three eight-year-old extras in *The Aliens Next Door*. What do you say?"

"Yes!" Nancy squealed. "Please, Dad, can we?"

Mr. Drew laughed. "Sounds like fun. George and Bess, I'll give your parents a call and see if it's okay with them."

"Yay!" The three girls cheered.

Mr. Banner opened his mouth to say something. But he was interrupted by a loud, horrible screech.

Nancy spun around. "What was that?" she cried out as something went tearing past them.

It was a cat. Nancy recognized her; it was Fluffington! Except Fluffington wasn't beautiful and fluffy and white, like she was in the Krunchies commercials. She was covered with blue paint!

CHAPTER THREE

You're Fired!

"Fluffington!" Mr. Banner shouted.

"Fluffington!" Yasmine shouted at the same time.

Fluffington skidded to a halt. She blinked up at Mr. Banner and Yasmine with her emerald-green eyes and let out a loud, angry meow.

Nancy stared in amazement at the famous cat. Fluffington's luxurious white fur was covered with gooey blue paint. She looked like an alien. She also looked bigger than Nancy remembered from the Krunchies commercials. Nancy wondered if she had been eating too many Krunchies lately.

"What in blazes is going on?" Mr. Banner demanded.

"Poor Fluffington," Bess murmured.

"She needs a bath!" Hannah said worriedly.

Yasmine scooped Fluffington up in her arms. She made a face as the gooey blue paint smeared onto her clothes and arms.

"She was supposed to be with the groomers, getting her beauty treatment," Yasmine told Mr. Banner. "I'll check with Patsy and see if she knows anything. Patsy!"

A young woman came rushing up to Yasmine and Mr. Banner. She was holding a brush in one hand and a towel in the other.

"Oh my gosh, I am so sorry," Patsy said breathlessly. "I was in the middle of grooming her. I turned my back for thirty seconds to get some supplies, and she was gone! What *happened*?" she gasped, taking in the sight of Fluffington's blue fur. "What did she get *into*?"

From behind a pile of boxes came a muffled

giggle. Nancy craned her head, trying to see who it was.

"Dad, I think someone's hiding behind there," Nancy whispered to her father, pointing.

Mr. Banner overheard her. He walked over to the boxes and peered behind them.

"Beezil!" Mr. Banner said angrily. "Come out here, right this second!"

A tall, skinny boy emerged. He had short, spiky brown hair, and his face was a sea of freckles. He looked like he was about twelve years old.

Nancy studied him closely. His hands and T-shirt were covered with blue paint!

"Hey, Dad," Beezil said to Mr. Banner, waving. *He's Mr. Banner's son,* Nancy thought.

"Explain yourself, Beezil," Mr. Banner demanded. "Why are you covered with blue paint? What did you do to Fluffington?"

"It's just stage makeup," Beezil said, rolling his eyes. "What's the big deal?"

"Do you know what you've done?" Mr. Banner shouted. "This is one prank too many, son. You're fired!"

"Fired?" Beezil repeated. "From what?"

"From this movie. You've demonstrated to me that you're not mature enough to have even a small acting part. Go to your, uh . . . go into my office and sit down and think about what you did," Mr. Banner ordered Beezil. "You're not allowed to use your cell phone or your game player for the rest of the day."

"Whatever," Beezil said sulkily. He walked into his father's office and closed the door behind him.

Wow, Mr. Banner just fired his own son, Nancy thought. *That's pretty serious!*

"I'll get Fluffington cleaned up," Patsy offered. She took the unhappy cat from Yasmine and hurried off.

"I think Fluffington's gaining weight. Maybe we should switch her to low-fat Krunchies," Yasmine called out after Patsy.

"I'm very sorry about all this," Mr. Banner apologized to Mr. Drew, Hannah, Nancy, George, and Bess. "You'll have to excuse me. I need to talk to my son. Carson, I know you and I have an appointment tomorrow afternoon to discuss business."

"Right," Mr. Drew said.

Mr. Banner turned to Nancy and her friends. "I'll have Yasmine take care of the paperwork for you to join our cast as extras. Maybe Carson or Hannah can bring you by here tomorrow morning around nine? We're shooting a crowd scene, and you three would be perfect for it."

"Sure!" Nancy, George, and Bess said in unison. They exchanged high fives.

Still, Nancy felt sorry for poor Fluffington. She hoped Patsy would be able to get all the blue paint off of her.

"Beezil's mom and Brett are divorced," said Meadow, who was one of the makeup artists. "Beezil's got some, uh, issues having to do with rules. As in, he doesn't like to follow them. Stay still, Nancy," she added.

Nancy obeyed. It was Tuesday morning, and she was sitting in one of the dressing rooms at Thunderchickens Studios. Meadow had already done George and Bess's hair and makeup. Now it was Nancy's turn.

Nancy's hair was in hot curlers; Meadow had

decided to style it into big, fluffy curls. Meadow was in the process of brushing Nancy's cheeks with pink powder.

Then Meadow smoothed pink lipstick onto Nancy's lips. Nancy crinkled her nose. Lipstick tasted really weird!

After Meadow finished with Nancy, the three girls were to be taken to an outdoor set near Soundstage #3. There Mr. Banner planned to shoot a crowd scene on the Mitchell family's "street"—not a real street, but a fake street with fake houses on it.

"Is Beezil an actor?" Bess asked Meadow.

"No way. His dad gave him a part in the movie—a really *small* part—because he needed to keep him busy," Meadow replied.

"Why does Mr. Banner need to keep Beezil busy?" George spoke up.

"Beezil's mom is in Europe for the summer," Meadow replied. "Mr. Banner is supposed to be taking care of him. Beezil had a babysitter for a while, but she quit after Beezil put a mouse in her backpack. The second babysitter quit after Beezil slipped shampoo into her smoothie. The third and fourth ones also quit. Mr. Banner finally gave up and started bringing Beezil to the set."

"Wow," Nancy said. *Beezil's a real trouble-maker,* she thought.

"Mr. Banner figured that giving Beezil a part in the movie would keep him in line." Meadow chuckled. "I guess not."

The dressing room door burst open. Yasmine rushed in.

"Have any of you seen her?" she demanded.

"Seen who, Yasmine?" Meadow said.

"Fluffington," Yasmine replied in an urgent-sounding voice.

Nancy, Bess, and George all shook their heads. "No. Why, Yasmine?" Meadow said curiously.

Yasmine frowned. She looked really worried.

"Fluffington is missing!" she announced.

CHAPTER FOUR

Where's Fluffington?

"Fluffington is missing?" Bess gasped.

"Maybe she just went for a walk or something," George suggested.

"I don't think so," Yasmine said anxiously. "No one's seen her in the last hour or so. It's not like Fluffington to disappear like that!"

"When was the last time anyone saw her?" Nancy asked Yasmine.

Yasmine looked thoughtful. "She was sitting in her usual place near the director's chair, eating her Krunchies breakfast. That's where she always gets fed. A couple of the wranglers, Jojo and Mikey, were with her."

"Wranglers?" Bess repeated, confused.

"Wranglers handle the animals on the set," Yasmine replied. "Jojo thought that Mikey was watching Fluffington, and Mikey thought that Jojo was watching her. During that time, Fluffington got away somehow. And now she's missing!" Yasmine added, "Everyone's looking for her, including Mr. Banner. He's superupset."

"We can help you guys look for her," Nancy offered. "We're good at finding missing people-and animals, too."

"Nancy, Bess, and I have a club called the Clue Crew," George explained. "We solve mysteries."

"That's great," Yasmine said gratefully. "We need all the help we can get."

"Fluffington!"

"Here, Fluffington!"

"Come here, Fluffy Wuffy cat!"

Nancy, George, and Bess were wandering around the back of the *Aliens* set, calling out Fluffington's name. They looked under set pieces. They looked under movie equipment.

They looked behind piles of boxes. Other people were searching for Fluffingto too, inside and outside.

Just then, Nancy got an idea. "I want to check out the place where Fluffington was having breakfast this morning."

"That's the last place where anyone saw Fluffington, right?" George said.

Nancy nodded. "Exactly. Maybe we can find some clues there."

The girls walked over to the director's chair, which was near the fake living room. The chair was black cloth on tall wooden legs that crisscrossed and made X's in front and back. The chair had the word "Director" written on it, in big white letters. *This is Mr. Banner's special chair for when he's directing a scene,* Nancy thought.

Near the director's chair was a big blue bowl with the word "Fluffington" on it, in gold. Nancy knelt down and peered into it. She could tell by a few tiny brown crumbs that it used to have Krunchies in it. Fluffington had obviously eaten

every last bite. There was also a water bowl.

George and Bess knelt down too. "Do you see any clues, Nancy?" George asked.

Nancy scanned the area carefully. "I don't see any-thing. If anyone kit-napped Fluffington from this spot, the person didn't leave any clues."

"Nice hairstyle. *Not.*"

Nancy turned around at the sound of the familiar voice. Beezil Banner was standing there. He gave Nancy a mean smile.

Nancy realized that Beezil was commenting on *her* hairstyle. She reached up and touched her hair. She was still wearing the hot curlers that Meadow had put there!

"What are you doing here?" Nancy asked Beezil. "I thought you were, uh—"

"Fired?" Beezil said. He set his backpack down on the ground and pulled a granola bar out of it. He unwrapped it and began chowing down on it with his mouth open.

"My dad will change his mind," Beezil went on. "He always does, about stuff like this. I know exactly how to make him do what I want him to do."

"Have you seen Fluffington?" Nancy asked him.

"She's missing, you know," George added.

"Maybe that dumb poodle Pow Wow or Pom-pom or whatever its name is ate her." Beezil cracked up at his joke.

Bess glared at him. "That's not funny."

Beezil shrugged. "You three are too young to appreciate my excellent sense of humor." He pulled a cell phone out of his pocket and flicked it open. "Gotta make a call. See you later. Bye,

Curlerhead," he added, grinning at Nancy.

"I don't like him," Bess whispered to Nancy and George after Beezil had disappeared around the corner.

"Me neither," George whispered back.

Just then, Nancy noticed a black backpack lying on the ground. It had the initials "BB" on it.

"Beezil left his backpack behind," Nancy told her friends. She walked over to it. She realized that if she hurried, she could catch up to Beezil and return it to him.

The backpack was unzipped at the top. Its contents caught Nancy's eye. She saw a couple of magazines, a balled-up red T-shirt, and some stinky socks. She made a face.

And then she noticed something else.

There was a plastic container full of something that looked like dried-up grass clippings. Nancy squinted to see the label. It said CATNIP.

"What is it, Nancy?" George asked her. "Did you find a clue?"

Nancy pointed out the catnip container to her friends. "Why would Beezil have catnip in his backpack?" she said in a low voice.

"Unless—," Bess began.

"Unless he used it to lure Fluffington away," Nancy finished. "Maybe Beezil is our *kit*-napper!"

ChaPTER FiVE

Another Prank?

"That's awful!" Bess cried out. "Why would Beezil kit-nap Fluffington?"

"We don't know that he did, for sure," Nancy said quickly. "It is kind of suspicious that he has catnip in his backpack, though."

"He could have kit-napped Fluffington to get back at his dad for firing him," George suggested.

Bess nodded. "Definitely. Or he could have kit-napped Fluffington as a dumb prank, like what he did with the blue stage paint." She added, "And didn't Meadow say he pulled a bunch of dumb pranks on his babysitters?"

"She said he put a mouse in his babysitter's

backpack. And he put shampoo in another babysitter's smoothie," Nancy recalled.

"When I'm old enough to babysit, I'm never, ever babysitting someone like Beezil!" Bess declared.

Nancy slung Beezil's backpack over her shoulder. "Let's go see what Beezil has to say about this."

The girls found Beezil hanging out in his father's office. He was sitting at Mr. Banner's desk and talking on his cell phone.

"Dude, you should have seen their faces when they found out!" Beezil was saying to the person on the other end. "They looked like they were going to—" He stopped when he noticed Nancy and her friends. "Yo, this is a private conversation. What do you want?"

Nancy lifted Beezil's backpack in the air. "You forgot something."

"I gotta go," Beezil mumbled into the phone. He snapped it shut and held out his hand. "Give it to me, Curlerhead," he said to Nancy.

"Not so fast. What are you doing with catnip?" Nancy asked him.

Beezil's cheeks flushed red. "You looked inside my bag? I'm telling my dad!"

"Your backpack was open," George said.

"You kitnapped Fluffington, didn't you, Beezil?" Bess accused him. "Why did you do it? Did you want to get back at your dad for firing you?"

"Wh-what?" Beezil sputtered. "What are you six-year-olds talking about?"

"We're eight," Nancy corrected him. "Did you use this catnip to lure Fluffington?"

"No way!" Beezil protested.

He got up from his father's desk and walked over to where Nancy and her friends were standing. He grabbed the backpack from Nancy and reached inside. "Look," he said, holding up the catnip container. "It's not even open. It's sealed shut with tape."

Nancy studied the container. Beezil was right.

"O-kay," she said slowly. "So maybe you had

two things of catnip, and you used the other one."

Beezil shook his head. "This is the only one. I bought it last night at a pet store. I wanted to give it to Fluffington, you know, because of, uh, what happened yesterday with the blue stage paint. I thought my dad would stop being mad at me if I gave Fluffington a present."

Nancy stared at Beezil. Was he telling the truth? It was hard to tell. Beezil was definitely a major troublemaker. But was he a liar, too?

Later that afternoon, Nancy leaned back in her beach chair and peered out over the top of her heart-shaped shades. The hotel pool—that is, the girls' favorite of the five hotel pools—was packed, mostly with kids. The pool area was landscaped with palm trees and tropical flowers that smelled like honey. Pink flamingos stood one-legged in the grass and preened their feathers.

George and Bess were sitting on either side of

Nancy. George was writing in a small spiral-bound notebook. Bess was brushing pretty pink polish on her toenails. Hannah was on the other side of Bess, leafing through a magazine.

Hannah glanced up. "Is the Clue Crew working on the Fluffington case?" she asked. Nancy and her friends had filled Hannah in on Fluffington's disappearance.

Nancy nodded. "George is writing down what we have so far."

"This is what I've got," George said, running her fingers down one of the pages in her

notebook. "*Clues,*" she read out loud. "Cat-nip in Beezil's backpack. *Suspects.* Beezil. He's a big fat troublemaker. He put blue paint on Fluffington the day before Fluffington disappeared. Plus he had the catnip."

"Beezil, Beezil, Beezil," Bess said. She brushed polish onto her right big toe. "It all points to Beezil. He must be our kit-napper!"

"We need to find more clues and suspects," Nancy pointed out.

"Don't forget about motive," George reminded Nancy and Bess. "If someone kit-napped Fluffington, then that person had to have a really good reason."

"Fluffington is a celebrity. The kit-napper could sell her for a lot of money. *That's* a motive," Bess said.

George wrote this down in her notebook. "There's also revenge," she said. "Maybe the kit-napper was really mad at Mr. Banner or someone else involved with *The Aliens Next Door.*"

"Those are both really good motives," Nancy said. "Or maybe the kitnapper had a motive that we haven't even thought about yet."

CHAPTER Six

A New Suspect

On Wednesday morning, Mr. Drew drove Nancy, George, and Bess to Thunderchickens Studios. The shooting of yesterday's crowd scene had been canceled due to Fluffington's disappearance. It had been rescheduled for today, even though Fluffington was still missing.

"The show must go on," Mr. Banner said to the cast and crew as they stood around, getting ready for the day. "We *will* find Fluffington. In the meantime, all we can do is act like the professionals we are and make the best movie possible. Come on, people, let's get to work!"

Everyone scattered. Mr. Drew walked over to

Mr. Banner. Nancy and her friends followed. Nancy noticed that Beezil wasn't around.

"Any news about Fluffington?" Nancy's dad asked Mr. Banner.

Mr. Banner shook his head. "I'm afraid not, Carson. I talked to the police this morning, and they're working on it. In the meantime, I'm trying to keep Fluffington's disappearance out of the newspapers. Otherwise—"

He lowered his voice. "Otherwise I'm going to have a lot of unhappy people on my hands. The president of Krunchies, Incorporated, for example. Also the *Aliens* producers, who have given us a lot of money to make this movie. And last but not least, Fluffington's owner, Mrs. Rice. She lives in New York City. She's very old. I don't think her health could take this kind of shock."

"What are you going to do?" Mr. Drew asked Mr. Banner. "About making the movie, I mean. You can't shoot Fluffington's scenes *without* Fluffington."

"Actually I can," Mr. Banner said.

"He's going to use that CG-something," Nancy spoke up.

Mr. Banner smiled at her. "Smart girl! That's right, Nancy. We'll use CGI—or 'computer generated imagery.' My CGI guy, Tucker Diaz, is working on it now. Nancy, George, Bess, you'd better go see Meadow for your hair and makeup. We're going to try to shoot that crowd scene in about an hour or so," he said.

"You girls better go," Mr. Drew said. "I'll pick you up at five so we can get ready for Pom-pom's birthday party tonight." He winked.

"Okay, Daddy," Nancy said. Mr. Banner had invited them to the celebrity dog's birthday party. Nancy had never been to a real Hollywood party. She couldn't wait!

Nancy hugged her dad good-bye. Then she, George, and Bess headed in the direction of the dressing room area.

On the way, they passed Tucker Diaz. He was working at his computer station. His face was

41

so close to his computer screen that his nose was almost touching it.

"Hi, Tucker," Nancy called out.

Tucker barely looked up. "What? Oh, hey. Hi, girls."

"Mr. Banner told us that you're superbusy," Bess said.

"Because of Fluffington being missing," George added.

Tucker yawned and rubbed his eyes. "I've been here since four a.m. trying to get these computer generated Fluffington images right," he said. "So? What do you think?"

He leaned back to let the girls see the computer screen. Nancy gasped. An image of Fluffington was on the screen. It looked just like her!

Then Tucker pressed some keys on his computer keyboard. The computer-Fluffington cleaned its whiskers with its paw. It chased a mouse. It jumped up in the air. It lay down and closed its eyes.

"That's amazing," Bess exclaimed. "It looks exactly like Fluffington!"

Tucker beamed. "It's like I've been trying to tell Mr. Banner. CGI is way better than the real thing. Now I finally have a chance to prove my point." He quickly added, "Not that I'm happy Fluffington is missing, of course."

Nancy frowned. *That was a strange thing for Tucker to say*, she thought.

Then Nancy noticed something even stranger.

Tucker had kitty hairs on his T-shirt. A *lot* of kitty hairs. He also had some scratches on both his arms.

Could they be kitty scratches? Nancy wondered. Could Tucker be Fluffington's kit-napper?

Nancy frowned. Tucker's scratches definitely could be kitty scratches. If he kit-napped Fluffington, then maybe Fluffington scratched him while she was trying to escape. *Poor Fluffington!* she thought.

Nancy tried to see if the kitty hairs on Tucker's T-shirt were white, like Fluffington's. But his T-shirt was light blue, so it was hard to make out the color of the kitty hairs. She needed to get a sample.

Nancy glanced around. She spotted a roll of tape on a nearby desk. She walked over to the desk, making sure Tucker wasn't watching, and very quietly tore off a piece of tape.

George stared at Nancy and mouthed the words, *What are you doing?* Nancy put her finger to her lips. She would explain everything to George and Bess later.

Nancy walked back to where Tucker was sitting. Bess was in the middle of asking Tucker a question. While Tucker answered, Nancy carefully placed the sticky part of the tape on his T-shirt. She made sure to aim for his sleeve, which was loose and baggy; that way, she wouldn't actually have to touch *him* and make him suspicious.

Just as carefully, she peeled the tape away from his sleeve. Something was stuck to the sticky part.

It was a bunch of long kitty hairs. Long *white* kitty hairs.

ChaPTER SEVEN

Bad News

The Paradise Beach Club was in a beautiful pink stone building overlooking the Pacific Ocean. Nancy, George, Bess, Hannah, and Mr. Drew arrived a little after seven o'clock. Nancy and her friends were wearing their best party dresses. The lobby was jammed with other guests, reporters, and photographers who pointed their flashing cameras at every passing person. There was a huge sign over the entranceway into the ballroom that said HAPPY THIRD BIRTHDAY, POMPOM!

"Wow," Nancy said, looking around.

"Double wow," George agreed.

They headed into the main ballroom. Nancy

spotted Mr. Banner nearby, talking to a group of reporters. Yasmine was standing next to him, holding Pompom in her arms. Pompom was wearing a beautiful jeweled collar and a white party hat. Nancy also recognized a bunch of cast and crew members from *The Aliens Next Door*.

"This is fancier than any human birthday party I've ever attended," Nancy's dad joked as a waiter offered him and Hannah a tray of tiny smoked salmon sandwiches.

"There's the kids' food!" Nancy said, pointing to a long white table decorated with balloons. "Can we check it out, Dad? Please?"

"Of course. Hannah and I will be right here, okay?" Mr. Drew sat down on a red velvet couch, and Hannah joined him.

Nancy grabbed George and Bess's hands, and the three of them rushed over to the kids' table. There were hot dogs, grilled cheese sandwiches, bagels, and fruit. There was also a platter of sugar cookies shaped like doggy bones.

Nancy and her friends prepared plates of

food and sat down at a small table with a palm-tree-shaped lamp on it. Nancy took a bite of her grilled cheese and glanced around. She spotted Tucker across the room.

"There's Tucker," Nancy whispered to George and Bess. Nancy had told them all about the white kitty hairs from Tucker's T-shirt as well as the kitty scratches on his arms. "We *have* to talk to him," she added.

"What are we going to ask him?" Bess whispered back. She pretended to confront Tucker. "'Hey, Tucker. How did you get those scratches on your arms? Did you get into a catfight with Fluffington while you were kit-napping her, or what?'"

"Something like that," Nancy said, grinning.

The girls finished their food and headed in Tucker's direction. On the way, they passed Mr. Banner talking to a reporter.

"Fluffington isn't here because she's not feeling well today," Mr. Banner was saying to the reporter. "I'm sure it's just a little kitty cold."

Nancy remembered what Mr. Banner had said to her dad, about not wanting people to find out that Fluffington had disappeared.

Nancy and her friends soon reached Tucker. "Hi, Tucker," Nancy said.

"Hi, girls," Tucker greeted them. "Enjoying the party?"

Bess put her hands on her hips. "Hey, Tucker. How did you get those scratches on your arms? Did you get into a catfight with Fluffington while you were kit-napping her, or what?" she blurted out.

"Bess!" Nancy cried out. She hadn't meant for her friend to say that *exactly*.

Tucker studied his arms. "Oh, these," he said casually. "I got these from my girlfriend's new kitten, Jellybean. Tara made me hold him, but he didn't really want to be held. I'm, uh, not really a cat person."

Nancy, George, and Bess exchanged glances. Nancy wondered if Tucker was telling the truth— or if he was lying. How could they be sure?

"Hey! Why are you asking me about kit-napping or kidnapping or whatever?" Tucker said suddenly. "You're not accusing me of having anything to do with Fluffington's disappearance, are you?"

Just then, a short woman with long black hair sauntered up to Tucker. "Hi, sweetie," she said, smiling at him.

"Hi, Tara. Tara, this is Nancy, George, and Bess. They're extras in *Aliens*. They were just asking me about Jellybean—," Tucker began.

Tara beamed. "That is so sweet of you girls to ask about my wittle wuv," she said, baby talking.

This gave Nancy an idea. "Do you have any photos of Jellybean?" she asked Tara.

Nancy wanted to see if Jellybean had long white fur, like Fluffington. If so, that could explain the long white cat hairs on Tucker's T-shirt.

"Do I have photos?" Tara exclaimed. "Do I ever!"

She reached into her metallic pink purse and pulled out a mini photo album. "This is Jellybean taking a nap," she said, flipping to the first photo.

Nancy saw right away that Jellybean had long white fur. But before she could thank Tara for showing them the photo, the young woman continued flipping through the album. "This is Jellybean eating breakfast," she recited. "This is Jellybean eating lunch. This is Jellybean eating dinner. This is Jellybean playing with his new catnip toy. This is Jellybean doing his business in his litter box."

She pouted and added, "I only wish Tucker and Jellybean liked each other. Tucker doesn't know how to hold her. Just last night, Tucker tried to pick her up, and he didn't do a very good job, and poor Jellybean was forced to defend himself."

Tucker held up his arms. "See? Didn't I tell you?" he said to Nancy, George, and Bess.

After a few more minutes and a lot more photos of Jellybean, the three girls thanked Tucker and Tara and said good-bye to them. Once they were out of earshot, Nancy leaned over to her friends. "I guess Tucker has a good explanation for the kitty scratches and kitty fur," she said in a low voice.

"Maybe," George said. "I'm still suspicious of him, though. He has a really good motive for wanting to kit-nap Fluffington."

"So he could make *Aliens* a CGI movie with no animal actors whatsoever," Bess added. "I agree with George. We should keep Tucker on our suspect list."

On Thursday morning, Nancy woke up in her hotel bed and rubbed her eyes. Bright sunlight streamed through the windows. She peered over at Bess and George in their beds. They were still asleep.

There was a knock on the door that led to the living room. "Who is it?" Nancy said. It was probably her father or Hannah. They were all sharing a three-bedroom suite, with the girls in one room, Mr. Drew in the second, and Hannah in the third.

The door cracked open. Mr. Drew poked his head inside. "Everyone awake?" he whispered.

"Shhh, Daddy! George and Bess are still asleep," Nancy whispered back.

"No, I'm not," came a voice from George's bed. Her blanket stirred.

"I'm not either," came a voice from Bess's bed. A foot with pretty pink toenails poked out from under her blanket.

Mr. Drew walked into the room. He was

dressed in pajamas and a robe. He was carrying a cup of coffee and a newspaper.

He held the newspaper out to Nancy. "There's something you need to see," he said in a serious voice. "It's related to your Clue Crew case."

Nancy took the newspaper from her father and unfolded it. The name of the newspaper was the *Hollywood Herald.*

Nancy scanned the front page and gasped. A headline in big, bold letters read:

ChaPTER, EighT

The Krunchies Klue

Nancy couldn't believe it. The *Hollywood Herald* had published an article about Fluffington!

There were three photographs that accompanied the article. There was one of Fluffington posing next to a bowl of Krunchies. There was one of Mr. Banner. And there was one of a woman with short, silver-blond hair. Her name was Felicity Katz.

Who's Felicity Katz? Nancy wondered.

"What's going on, Nancy?" George said curiously. She got into bed beside Nancy and peered over her shoulder. Bess got into bed on the other side, holding her teddy bear. Mr.

Drew sat down in an armchair and took a sip of his coffee.

The three girls read the article together:

HOLLYWOOD—Celebrity feline Fluffington disappeared mysteriously from Thunderchickens Studios on Tuesday morning.

The Krunchies spokes-cat was in the middle of shooting her first film, *The Aliens Next Door*, directed by Brett Banner.

According to an anonymous source close to the movie, Fluffington was "probably kidnapped by someone who wants to sell her on the black market for a lot of money."

Felicity Katz, president of the Fluffington Fan Club, was visibly upset when she heard the news. "America's favorite feline must be found!" she declared.

Mr. Banner would not comment on this story.

Nancy glanced up from the newspaper. "How did the reporter find out about Fluffington?" she said, stunned.

Bess jabbed her finger at the article. "It says something about an 'anonymous source close to the movie.' Who could that be?"

"Maybe it's that mean, nasty Beezil," George suggested.

"Or maybe it's someone we don't even know," Nancy mused. "We haven't met *every-one* at the studio."

Mr. Drew glanced at his watch. "Speaking of which, I need to head over to the studio very soon. Brett called and wanted me to look over some—"

"Can we go with you, Daddy?" Nancy burst out. "I think this is a good time for the Clue Crew to look around for more clues."

"Definitely," George agreed.

"As long as we get some breakfast first," Bess said, hugging her teddy bear to her chest.

Nancy's dad smiled. "Okay. Breakfast first, then off we go to Thunderchickens Studios."

Everyone at Thunderchickens Studios was buzzing about the *Hollywood Herald* article when Nancy, George, Bess, and Mr. Drew got there. Mr. Banner was pacing up and down the hallway in front of his office, barking into his cell phone. "How did this happen? Who leaked this to the reporters? I want to know *now!*"

He hung up as soon as he spotted Mr. Drew. "Carson! I need to talk to you ASAP."

"I'm all yours, Brett," Mr. Drew said. "These girls want to look around the studio, if that's okay with you. They've been working very hard to try to help find Fluffington."

"Young detectives. How wonderful!" Mr. Banner said, beaming. "Look around all you want, girls. Let me know if you need anything."

"Thanks, Mr. Banner," Nancy said.

Mr. Banner led Mr. Drew into his office and

closed the door. "Now what?" George said to Nancy and Bess.

"Now we start looking for clues," Nancy replied. "We should look in all the places where we didn't look before."

"Sounds like a good plan," Bess agreed.

Nancy glanced around. She decided to start with the hallway, to the right. She thought there were some rooms in that direction that the Clue Crew hadn't searched yet.

While they walked, George pulled her spiral-bound notebook out of her pocket and flipped to a page. "So far, we have three clues: the catnip we found in Beezil's backpack, the long white kitty hairs on Tucker's T-shirt, and the kitty scratches on Tucker's arms," she recited.

Nancy peeked behind a potted plant. She remembered seeing the big yellow stray cat, Honey Mustard, hanging out near it the other day. "There are no clues back here," she said.

"Hey, what's this?" Bess called over her shoulder. She had hurried ahead.

Nancy and George caught up to Bess. She was standing in the doorway of a small storage room. She pointed to a green wooden door on the far side of the room. The door was marked EXIT in faded letters.

Nancy hurried over to the door. She stood close to it and inspected it. There were scratches on both the door and the door frame. Nancy's pulse quickened. They looked like kitty scratches!

She pointed out the scratches to George and Bess. "Maybe Fluffington scratched the door until it opened wide enough for her to escape," she guessed.

"I bet that's what happened!" exclaimed Bess.

Nancy opened the door slowly. Something caught her eye. There was a small red bowl on the ground, containing a single brown kibble.

"It looks like a Krunchies kibble," Nancy noted.

Bess frowned. "I don't get it. I thought Fluffington always got fed in her special blue bowl by the director's chair. That's what Yasmine told us, remember?"

"I remember," Nancy said.

Nancy looked around. Across from where they stood was another building, surrounded by palm trees.

Mounted on top of the building was a camera, a security camera.

Thinking quickly, Nancy ran a few feet to the right. Then she skipped a few feet to the left.

"Nancy, what are you doing?" Bess asked her, giggling. "Are you exercising, or what?"

Nancy pointed to the security camera, which was moving back and forth in sync with her movements. "It's following me," she said. "It's a . . . it's a . . ." She paused, trying to remember exactly what the device was called. "It's a motion-sensitive security camera—or something like that."

"Cool," George said. "But why are you playing games with it, Nancy? We have to look for more clues!"

Nancy smiled. "It *is* a clue, George. If Fluffington escaped through this green door, or if someone kit-napped her from this spot, the security camera might have taken a picture of it!"

CHAPTER NINE

Closing In

"Next tape!" Nancy called out.

"I think this is our third tape," George remarked.

"It's kind of boring watching the same green door for hours and hours, with nothing happening," Bess added, yawning.

The three girls were sitting in Mr. Banner's office with Mr. Banner, Yasmine, and Mr. Drew. They were watching videotapes on the director's large screen TV.

But they weren't just *any* videotapes. They were the videotapes from the special security camera Nancy had discovered—the one across from the green door of Soundstage #3. The tapes were all from Tuesday morning, when Fluffington disappeared.

"It's very clever of you girls to come up with the idea of watching these tapes," Mr. Banner said.

Another image of the green door flashed across the TV screen. The tapes were only video, no audio, which meant there was no sound.

Then the image of the green door twitched. Something was happening. A woman appeared on the TV screen. She had short, silver-blond hair. Nancy frowned. She looked familiar.

The woman kneeled down by the green door. She set a red bowl on the ground and poured some kibbles into it from a plastic bag. Then she rattled the bowl, as if trying to make a noise with it.

"Oh my gosh!" Bess burst out. "Maybe she's Fluffington's kit-napper!"

All of a sudden, Nancy knew why the woman looked familiar. "That's Felicity Katz," she said excitedly. "Her picture was in this morning's

Hollywood Herald. She's the president of the Fluffington Fan Club—right, Mr. Banner?"

"Oh, yes, *her*," Mr. Banner said. "What is she doing on the studio grounds? How did she get past the security guards?"

Nancy watched the TV screen intently. A moment later, the green door opened ever so slightly. A paw reached out.

A fluffy white paw.

On the TV screen, Felicity Katz glanced

over her shoulder, as if to make sure no one was looking. Then she opened the green door wider. A fluffy white cat rushed out—and headed right for the bowl!

"Fluffington!" Mr. Banner exclaimed.

"Felicity Katz is definitely the kit-napper," George said.

Then the image twitched. A truck appeared on the screen. After a few minutes, the truck drove away. The image of the green door appeared again.

Felicity Katz—and Fluffington—were gone.

"The security camera was paying attention to the truck, so we don't know what happened to Ms. Katz and Fluffington," Nancy said, disappointed.

Mr. Banner turned to Yasmine. "Call the police. I want them to arrest Felicity Katz ASAP!" he barked.

Nancy stood up. "Wait, Mr. Banner. We don't have any proof that Ms. Katz actually kit-napped Fluffington. We only have proof that she fed her Krunchies." She added, "I think we should talk to her first. If you can get her here, I think I know what to do."

Mr. Banner seemed to consider this. "Okay," he said finally. "But if she doesn't give us the information we need, I'm definitely calling the police."

"I was so, so pleased to get your phone call asking me to help you find Fluffington," Felicity Katz said to Mr. Banner as she sat down across the desk from him. "I'm happy to do whatever I can to locate America's favorite feline!"

Nancy studied Felicity Katz. She looked just like she did in the *Hollywood Herald* photo and the security videotape. Today, she was dressed in a Fluffington T-shirt and jeans. She carried a cat-shaped purse and wore a chunky necklace made of cat-shaped beads. Matching cat-shaped earrings dangled from her ears.

Nancy, George, Bess, and Mr. Drew were in

Mr. Banner's office. They had all waited there for Felicity Katz to arrive.

"So what can I do?" Ms. Katz said eagerly. "I have a website devoted to Fluffington. I know everything there is to know about her."

"You can start out by watching a little TV," Mr. Banner said.

Ms. Katz frowned. "What? I'm sorry, I don't understand."

Mr. Banner turned to Nancy. "Go ahead."

Nancy picked up the remote control and switched on the TV set. The image of Ms. Katz flashed across the screen. She poured

Krunchies into the red bowl, and a moment later, Fluffington appeared.

"Stop that!" Ms. Katz cried out. "I can explain everything!"

"You kit-napped Fluffington, didn't you?" Bess burst out. "Why did you do it, Ms. Katz?"

Ms. Katz shook her head. "No, no. It wasn't like that at all. You see, I was just trying to get a paw-tograph of Fluffington. I snuck past the security guard at the front gate while he was on a phone call. I managed to lure Fluffington out of that green door using Krunchies. My goodness, Fluffington has a big appetite! Frankly, you people need to think about putting her on a little diet."

She added, "Anyway, when I tried to pick her up for the paw-tographing process, she wouldn't let me. She hissed at me—can you imagine? *Me*, her number one fan! Then she got distracted by a huge yellow creature in the bushes. The two of them ran off somewhere."

"You're making this up," Mr. Banner accused her. "It's the craziest story I've ever heard. A paw-tograph? What is that, anyway?"

"An autograph of Fluffington's paw," Ms. Katz explained patiently. "I brought the ink with me and everything. Vegetable based ink, I might add. I wanted to make sure it would be safe for Fluffington's delicate tummy—well, Fluffington's delicate but very *large* tummy."

Nancy was silent as she thought over Ms. Katz's story. Was the fan club president telling the truth? Or was she spinning a tall tale to cover up her kit-napping crime?

One of the details in Ms. Katz's story tugged at Nancy's brain. "Did you say something about a huge yellow creature?" she asked Ms. Katz.

Ms. Katz nodded. "A huge yellow cat. Fluffington and this cat seemed to be best friends or something. Fluffington and the cat did nose kisses when they saw each other. And then they ran off down the road."

Nancy considered this.

"I think I know how to find Fluffington!" she announced.

CHAPTER TEN

It's a Wrap!

Everyone stared at Nancy. "How can we find Fluffington?" Mr. Banner asked her. "If you have any brilliant ideas, please share them with us!"

"I think the yellow cat is Honey Mustard," Nancy began. "Yasmine told George, Bess, and me that he hangs out at the studio sometimes. It sounds like Fluffington went somewhere with Honey Mustard on Tuesday morning. Which means that if we can find Honey Mustard, we might be able to find Fluffington."

"Sounds like a plan, Nancy," Mr. Drew told her.

"Yes, it sounds like a *marvelous* plan!" Ms.

Katz exclaimed. "Let's begin immediately. How can I help?"

"I think we should have a two part strategy," Nancy suggested. "First we should set out lots of bowls of Krunchies inside and out, to try to lure Honey Mustard. Honey Mustard is a stray, so he doesn't have an owner who feeds him. He might be hungry."

"Poor little guy," Bess said sympathetically. "Poor *big* guy, I mean."

"Second, a bunch of us should spread out and search for Honey Mustard inside and outside," Nancy went on. "Yasmine told us that he has six toes on each paw. So we should be on the lookout for any paw prints with six toes."

Mr. Banner nodded. "I'll get the cast and crew together. We'll organize a massive search team to look for Honey Mustard."

"Here, Honey Mustard!"

"Here, yellow kitty!"

"Here, Honey Wunny Mustard Bear!"

Nancy, George, and Bess called out for Honey Mustard as they peered behind some flower bushes. Mr. Drew was nearby, looking inside a storage shed. The four of them had been looking for Honey Mustard for the last hour. There were dozens of other search teams as well, scouring the grounds of Thunderchickens Studios.

They had searched the outside of several soundstages and warehouses. They had searched under dozens of parked cars. But they had found no sign of Honey Mustard—or Fluffington, for that matter.

They continued down the narrow road that wound through the studio grounds. They soon reached a dirt path that branched off from the road.

Nancy noticed something on the path. "Look!" she cried out.

"What is it, Nancy?" George asked her.

Nancy pointed to a series of paw prints on the dusty path—and counted. "One, two, three, four, five, six! There are six toes on each paw!"

"Let's follow the paw prints and see if they lead us to Honey Mustard—and Fluffington, too," Nancy said. She lowered her voice. "Let's be superquiet. If the kitties are out there some-where, we don't want to scare them away."

Bess, George, and Mr. Drew nodded. The four of them continued down the dusty path, following the paw prints.

The path led through a grove of palm trees and into a clearing. In the middle of the clearing was a tugboat. The tugboat was small and looked very old, with chipping white paint and faded blue trim. The tugboat's name was inscribed on its side; it was *Fish Party*.

"I wonder if this boat was in a movie," Nancy whispered.

A tiny sound came from the boat. Nancy strained, trying to hear. It sounded like a bird.

The sound came again—and again.

That's not a bird, Nancy thought.

She rushed up to the tugboat and peeked inside. George, Bess, and Mr. Drew followed her. "What is it?" Bess whispered.

Nancy gasped at the sight that greeted her.

Inside the boat were Fluffington and Honey Mustard. They were curled up on some old life preservers.

Curled up next to Fluffington were six tiny kittens!

Three of the kittens were fluffy and white, just

like Fluffington. The other three were yellow—
the same color as Honey Mustard.

"Fluffington's a mom!" George cried out.

"And Honey Mustard's a dad," Mr. Drew
added with a chuckle.

The kittens continued making their tiny
mewling noises. Fluffington gave each of them
a bath by licking them with her pink tongue.

Nancy smiled. Fluffington had disappeared so
she could give birth to her kittens. Nancy remembered that pregnant cats like to go off on their
own, away from humans, and "nest" right before
giving birth. Fluffington's
nest had been some
life preservers

inside a tugboat called *Fish Party*. This also explained why she had been such a big kitty!

The Clue Crew solves another mystery, Nancy thought happily. She couldn't wait to share the good news with Mr. Banner and everyone else back at the studio.

"Cut!" Mr. Banner shouted. "Great scene, kids! That's a wrap!"

Nancy, George, and Bess turned to each other and exchanged high fives. Mr. Banner had just finished shooting an outdoor scene.

To thank the girls for finding Fluffington, he had given each of them one line of dialogue to say. Nancy's line had been: "Did you see that?" George's line had been: "It looked like an alien from outer space!" Bess's line had been: "There's no such thing as aliens!" So in the end, they had gotten to be more than extras in a crowd scene. They had gotten to be real actors!

Nancy loved being in a Hollywood movie. *Acting is almost as fun as solving mysteries,* she thought.

Mr. Drew and Hannah came up to Nancy and her friends and gave them big hugs. They had been watching from the sidelines. "You're movie stars now," Hannah said.

"Can I have your autographs?" Nancy's dad joked.

Nancy giggled. "Sure, Daddy."

Just then, Fluffington trotted up to Nancy and rubbed up against her ankle, purring. Nancy reached down to pet her. Then Fluffington trotted off to join Honey Mustard and their six kittens. The Fluffington-Honey Mustard family shared a cozy new kitty bed now, right next to the director's chair.

Nancy was so glad that she, George, and Bess had found Fluffington, Honey Mustard, and their babies, safe and sound. She was also glad that she had solved another piece of the mystery: the identity of the person who had talked to the *Hollywood Herald* about Fluffington. The culprit had been Beezil. Nancy had overheard him bragging about it to a friend on his cell phone. It looked like Beezil hadn't changed his troublemaking ways at all.

"If the movie stars aren't too tired, would they be interested in some pizza?" Mr. Drew said to Nancy and her friends. "I'm treating!"

"Yes!" Nancy, George, and Bess said all together.

"Meow!" Fluffington and Honey Mustard cried. Nearby, Pompom barked.

Nancy laughed. It was a perfect Hollywood ending!

Throw a Hollywood Movie Party for Your Friends!

Invite your friends to a "Hollywood premiere"— at your house!

You Will Need:

Plain postcards and envelopes

Magic Markers

Small gold and silver star stickers

Stamps for mailing

A red tablecloth roll (this is a disposable, or throw-away, tablecloth that is sold in rolls of 40 inches by 100 feet or a size close to that)

Black permanent marker

Duct tape or other heavy tape

A piece of cardboard cut into the shape of star (make the star as big as your hand or bigger)

Gold and silver craft paper or gift-wrapping paper

Scissors

Clear tape

One or more DVDs or videos to show on your TV set

A glitzy costume so you can dress up as your fave movie star

Fun snacks, like popcorn served in plastic top hats; pizza served on fancy silver trays; and soda or juice served in plastic champagne glasses

Optional: A regular camera or disposable cameras; a video camera (if it's okay with your parents); a costume trunk; sparkly holiday lights to hang in your TV room; gold, silver, black, and white balloons; a toy microphone

To Make the Invitations

❀ Using Magic Markers, write WALK THE RED CARPET TO [YOUR NAME'S] HOLLYWOOD PARTY! on plain postcards and decorate them with gold and silver star stickers. Make sure to include your address, date, and time. If you want, invite your guests to dress up as a Hollywood actor or actress.

❀ Put the invitations in envelopes, decorate them with more star stickers, and mail. Make sure to do this at least a week before your party.

To Make the Red Carpet

❀ On the day of the party, roll out the red plastic tablecloth. You can do this outside your house so the "carpet" leads to your front door; or you can do this inside your house so the "carpet" leads to your TV room.

❀ With your parents' help, tape the red carpet down with duct tape or other heavy tape so it doesn't move or blow away.

❀Using black permanent marker, carefully trace star shapes on the red carpet with your star-shaped cardboard. When your guests arrive, you can invite them to write their names inside the stars!

To Decorate Your "Screening Room"

❀ Take the star-shaped cardboard that you used for the red carpet and trace star shapes onto gold and silver craft or wrapping paper. Cut out the shapes, write your guests' names inside the stars, and tape up the stars on the walls of your TV room.

❀ You can also decorate the TV room with sparkly holiday lights and balloons.

It's Time to Have Fun!

❀ As your guests arrive, invite them to write their names on the red carpet, inside the stars. If you want, you (or a friend or family member) can take photos of the arriving guests or film them with a video camera.

❀ Once in your "screening room," serve your yummy movie snacks. If you have a toy microphone, you can call out your guests' names, like they do on the Oscars ("It looks like TV actress Rachel Wagner is here with her sister Bethany!"). If you have a costume trunk, your guests can try on different oufit combos. If you have disposable cameras, pass them out so everyone can go snap-crazy!

❀ When you're all ready to watch the movie, pop in a DVD or video and dim the lights. It's showtime!